Mckittrick

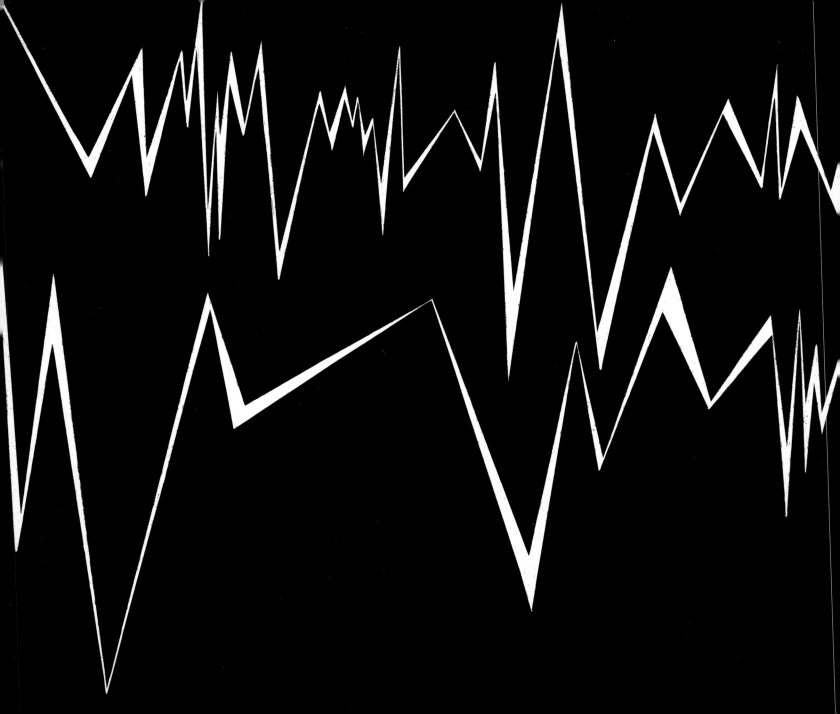

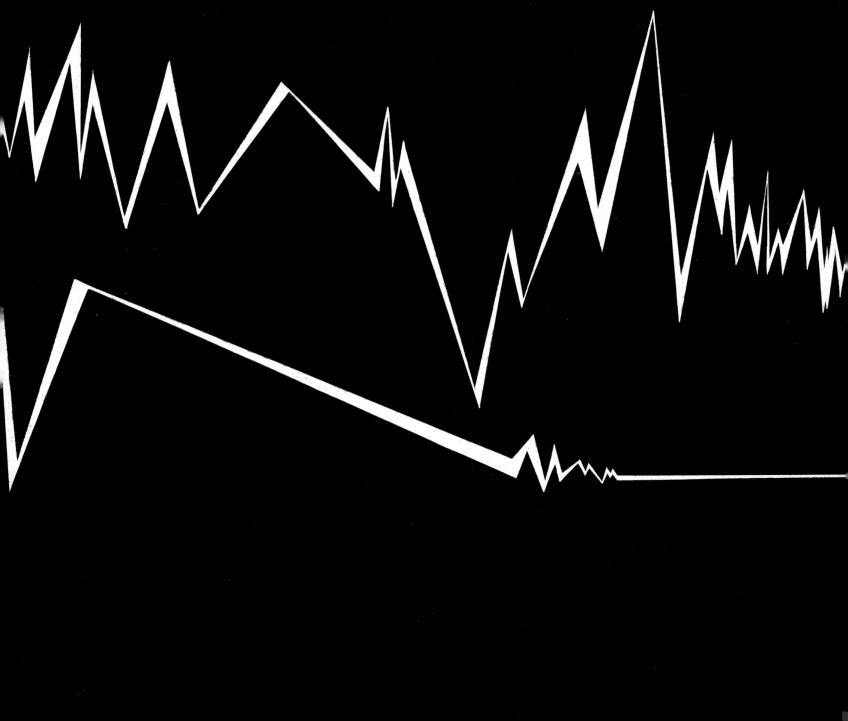

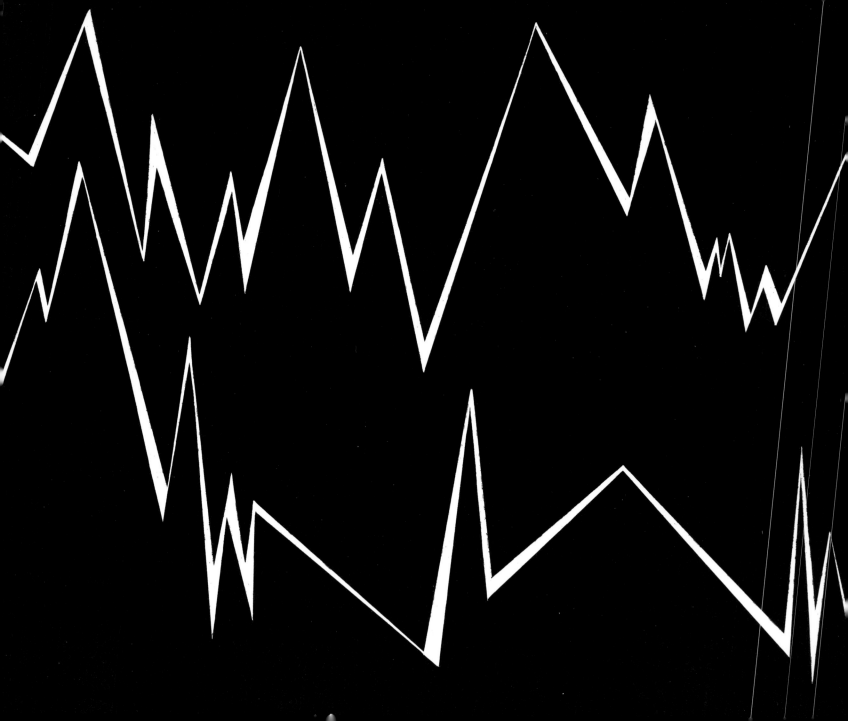

Ben's Trumpet

by RACHEL ISADORA

GREENWILLOW BOOKS
A DIVISION OF WILLIAM MORROW & COMPANY, INC.
NEW YORK

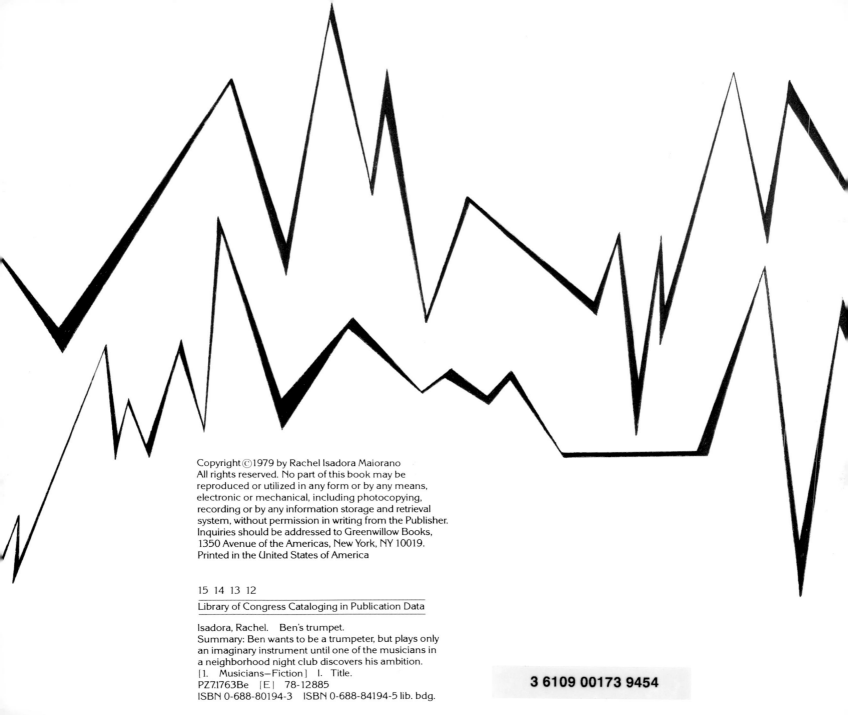

15 14 13 12

Library of Congress Cataloging in Publication Data

Isadora, Rachel.   Ben's trumpet.
Summary: Ben wants to be a trumpeter, but plays only
an imaginary instrument until one of the musicians in
a neighborhood night club discovers his ambition.
[1. Musicians—Fiction] I. Title.
PZ7.I763Be [E] 78-12885
ISBN 0-688-80194-3   ISBN 0-688-84194-5 lib. bdg.

In the evening, Ben sits on the fire escape and
listens to the music from the Zig Zag Jazz Club.
He joins in, playing his trumpet. Sometimes he plays
until very late and falls asleep in the hot night air.

Every day on the way home from school,
Ben stops by the Zig Zag Jazz Club.

He watches the musicians practice.

The pianist,

the saxophonist,

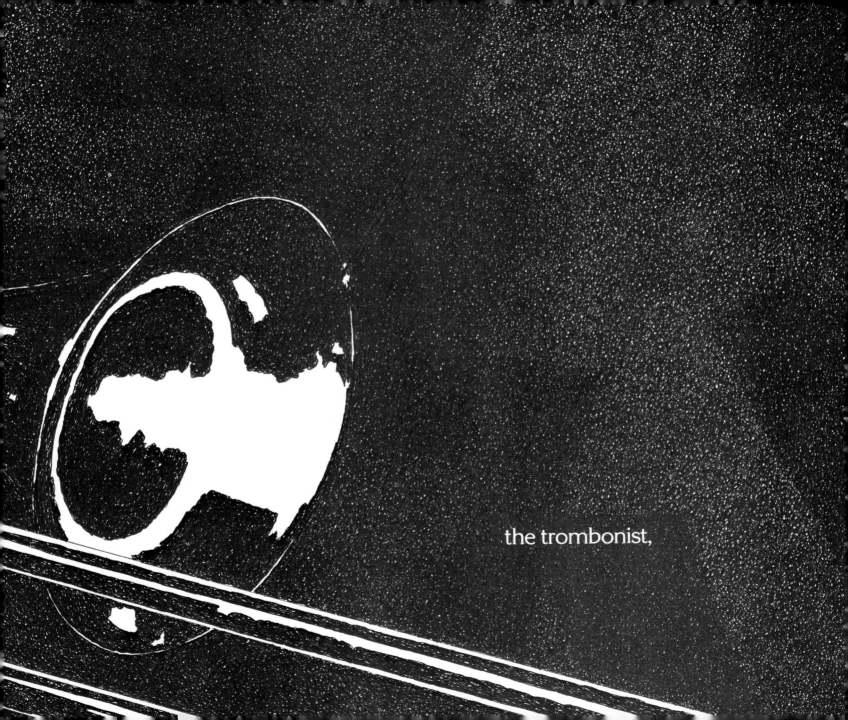

the trombonist,

and the drummer.

But most of all Ben thinks the trumpeter is the cat's meow.

Ben feels the rhythm of the
music all the way home.

He plays for his mama,
grandmother and
baby brother.

And for his papa and his friends.

One day, Ben is sitting on the stoop
and playing his trumpet.
"I like your horn," someone says.

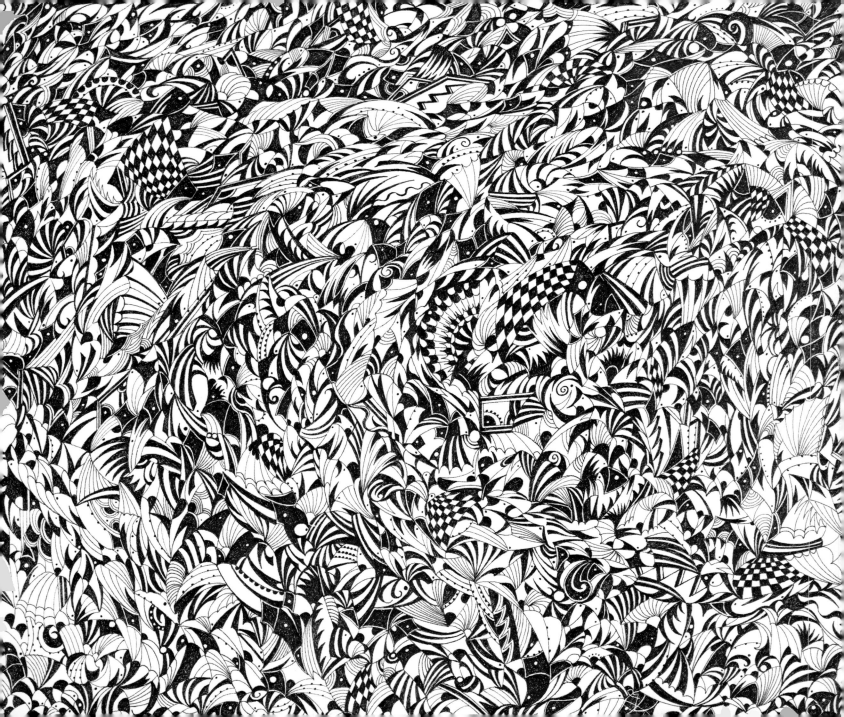

It is the trumpeter from the Zig Zag Jazz Club!
Ben smiles and watches him walk to the Club.

The next day, after school, Ben stops and listens
to the musicians practicing a red hot piece.
He starts blasting away at his trumpet.
Some kids in front of the candy store watch him.
"Hey, what ya doing?" they yell.

Ben stops and turns around.
"What ya think ya doing?" they ask again.
"I'm playing my trumpet," Ben answers.
"Man, you're crazy! You got no trumpet!"
They laugh and laugh.

Ben puts his hands in his pockets
and walks slowly home.

Down the street the band comes out for a break.
  The trumpeter comes over to Ben.
"Where's your horn?" he asks.
"I don't have one," Ben says.
  The trumpeter puts his hand on Ben's shoulder.
"Come on over to the club," he says,